Henry and Mudge
AND THE
Sneaky Crackers

The Sixteenth Book of Their Adventures

Story by Cynthia Rylant
Pictures by Suçie Stevenson

ALADDIN PAPERBACKS

For Aaron Mancini—CR

For Leo Stevenson—SS

THE HENRY AND MUDGE BOOKS

First Aladdin Paperbacks edition February 1999

Text copyright © 1998 by Cynthia Rylant
Illustrations copyright © 1998 by Suçie Stevenson

Aladdin Paperbacks
An imprint of Simon & Schuster
Children's Publishing Division
1230 Avenue of the Americas
New York, NY 10020

READY-TO-READ is a registered trademark of Simon & Schuster, Inc.

Also available in a Simon & Schuster Books for Young Readers edition.
Manufactured in the United States of America

20 19

The Library of Congress has cataloged the hardcover edition as follows:
Rylant, Cynthia.
Henry and Mudge and the sneaky crackers : the sixteenth book of their adventures /
by Cynthia Rylant ; illustrated by Suçie Stevenson.
p.   cm. — (The Henry and Mudge books) (Ready-to-read) "Level 2"—Spine.
Summary: While trying out the spy glasses, spy hat, and other items in their new spy kit,
seven-year-old Henry and his dog Mudge make a new friend and form a spy club.
ISBN-13: 978-0-689-81176-0 (hc.)
ISBN-10: 0-689-81176-4 (hc.)
[1. Dogs—Fiction. 2. Spies—Fiction. 3. Clubs—Fiction.]
I. Stevenson, Suçie, ill. II. Title. III. Series. IV. Series: Rylant, Cynthia. Henry and Mudge books.
PZ7.R982Heao   1998
[E]—dc21   96-44986
ISBN-13: 978-0-689-82525-5 (pbk.)
ISBN-10: 0-689-82525-0 (pbk.)

Contents

The Spy Kit

Henry and Henry's big dog Mudge
liked to watch a TV show
called *The Man in the Mask*.
It was about a spy.
Henry loved spies.

One day he saw
a spy kit for sale.
"Mudge, let's get the
piggy bank," said Henry.

Henry emptied the bank
and bought the kit.

It was great.

There was a spy hat and spy glasses.

There was a spy telescope.

There was a secret code
on a secret card.

And, best of all,
there was a magnifying glass.

Henry looked at Mudge
through the
magnifying glass.
"We're spies now, Mudge,"
Henry said.
Mudge wagged.

"We'll flirt with
danger,"
Henry said.
Mudge wagged again.
"And steal secrets,"
said Henry.

Mudge wagged harder.

He was ready to be a spy.

He gave the magnifying glass

a big wet lick.

Henry looked at the

drooly glass.

"Hmm," said Henry.

"Maybe you should

just wear the hat."

Code!

Henry put the spy glasses
on himself and
the spy hat on Mudge
and they went outside.

They walked down
the street, spying.

"Try not to look
like you're spying, Mudge,"
Henry said.
Mudge rolled
around in a puddle.
"Hmm," said Henry. "Good job."

Henry looked through

his magnifying glass.

Suddenly he saw something suspicious.

"This way, Mudge,"

he said.

They sneaked behind a bush.

They zipped between
some trash cans.

"Hey, look at this, Mudge,"
said Henry.

He held his magnifying glass
over a piece of paper on the ground.
He read: E3T 27Q 5TB
"Code!" said Henry.

But Mudge wasn't listening.

He was spying.

He was spying
an old shoe
in one of the trash cans.

Mudge loved old shoes.

"No, Mudge," said Henry.

"Nasty can."

Mudge chewed on a big
rock instead.
"You're doing
a good job not
looking like a spy,"
said Henry,
patting Mudge's head.
Mudge wagged and spit out the rock.
Spying was fun!

Crackers

Henry took the code
back home.
"It's a message, Mudge,"
Henry said.
"And we have to crack it."

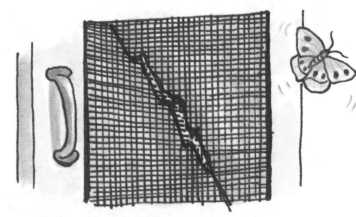

Mudge wagged.

He was good at cracking things.

There were things all over the house

that Mudge

had cracked.

Henry took out the
secret code card.
He held it next
to the message.
Carefully he began working.

Since Mudge couldn't
eat the code
or lick the code
or roll over on the code,
he decided to sleep.
He lay and snored,
waiting to flirt with danger.

Finally Henry cracked the code.

"I've got it!" he said.

"See?"

Mudge opened one eye.

"It says, 'Who are you?'"

Mudge opened both eyes.

"Wow!" said Henry. "Another spy!"

For a week Henry left
secret messages by the
trash cans.

And for a week Henry
picked up secret messages
by the trash cans.
Mudge chewed a lot of rocks.
Finally Henry left a message
that said, "Meet me here 5:00 Monday."

And a boy holding the
same spy kit met him
on Monday!
The boy also had a dog,
who was also wearing a hat.

"Wow!" said Henry. "Let's be a club."
Because they were so good
at cracking codes,
the boys named their club
"Crackers."

And for ID,
they always carried some
real crackers
in their pockets.
Did Mudge ever love THAT!